Don't count the number of birthdays. Count how happy you feel. I'm Birthday Bear, and I'll help make your birthdays the best ever.

I'm Wish Bear, and if you wish on my star, maybe your special dream will come true.

If you're ever feeling lonely, just call on me, Friend Bear. See, I've got a daisy for you and a daisy for me.

Grr! I'm Grumpy Bear. There's a cloud on my tummy to show that I take the grouchies away, so you can be happy again.

I'm Love-a-Lot Bear. I have two hearts on my tummy. One is for you; the other is for someone you love.

It's my job to bring you sweet dreams. I'm Bedtime Bear, and right now I'm a bit sleepy. Are you sleepy, too?

Now that you know all of us, we hope that you'll have a special place for us in your heart, just like we do for you.

With love from all of us,

♥

The Care Bears

Published in the United States by Parker Brothers, Division of CPG Products Corp.

Care Bears, Care Bears Logo, Tenderheart Bear, Friend Bear, Grumpy Bear, Birthday Bear, Cheer Bear, Bedtime Bear, Funshine Bear, Love-a-Lot Bear, Wish Bear and Good Luck Bear are trademarks of American Greetings Corporation, Parker Brothers, authorized user.

Library of Congress Cataloging in Publication Data: Rosenblatt, Arthur S. The Care Bears battle the freeze machine. A Tale from the Care Bears. SUMMARY: The Care Bears foil Professor Coldheart's plan to use his Care-less Ray contraption that can turn its victims into blocks of ice.
[1. Friendship—Fiction. 2. Bears—Fiction] I. Title. II. Series.
PZ7.R71916Car 1984 [E] 83-24955 ISBN 0-910313-15-6
Manufactured in the United States of America   4 5 6 7 8 9 0

A Tale from the
Care Bears

The Care Bears Battle the Freeze Machine

Story by Arthur S. Rosenblatt
Pictures by Joe Ewers

It was a typical day in the land of Care-a-Lot.

Baby Hugs was chasing a floating bumblebee.
Baby Tugs was busy licking honey off his paw.
When he saw Hugs approach the edge of the cloud,
he shouted, "I'll save you, Baby Hugs." In his
hurry, Baby Tugs tripped and went sliding toward
the edge of the cloud himself.

Luckily Grams Bear was nearby, and she caught both Baby Bears at once. "Now you two rascals just settle yourselves down," she warned. "You're not grown-up Care Bears yet, you know."

"But I will be soon," answered Baby Tugs as he tried to stand up taller.

On a nearby cloud Tender Heart Bear was turning his telescope toward the town below. "Do you see anyone who needs help?" Wish Bear asked.

"I think I'm about to," Tenderheart Bear said.

Sure enough, trouble was beginning outside
the hardware store. A big, tough boy had
gathered a group around him. "Hey, Lumpy, what
are you going to do?" asked one of the other boys.
"Just wait and see," the big boy answered.

The door opened, and a small boy stepped outside. He was carrying a big bag full of hardware.

"Here's how we get 'brainy boy' Paul," Lumpy said as he shoved his bat between Paul's feet.

Paul tripped. The bag fell to the ground, and out spilled a collection of nuts and bolts, wire and springs.

Paul looked at the bat and said, "You did that
on purpose. Why are you always picking on me?"

    " 'Cause you're an oddball, and we don't like oddballs," answered Lumpy. Then he and the others laughed and ran off to the playground.

    "I'll get even with you! You just wait and see," shouted Paul after them.

From a nearby alleyway, an odd-looking man had watched what had happened at the hardware store. It was the Mad Scientist, Professor Cold Heart. Sitting on his Ice-cycle, he smiled coldly. "Hee, hee, hee, I love to see kids playing mean tricks. Too bad I can't stay to see more, but I have bigger plans."

In Care-a-Lot, Tenderheart Bear said, "I think Paul needs some Care Bear care."

"Before things get out of hand," said Wish Bear.

Grumpy Bear jumped up and said, "Grr! If that Cold Heart is around, Paul needs some help right now."

Cheer Bear shouted, "OK, Care Bears. Into your Cloud Cars and Rainbow Racers!"

As the Care Bears started to take off, Baby Tugs jumped into the back of Tenderheart's Cloud Car. "Come on, Hugs, this is our chance to go on a Care Bear adventure." None of the other Care Bears saw them as he pulled Hugs into the car, and away they went.

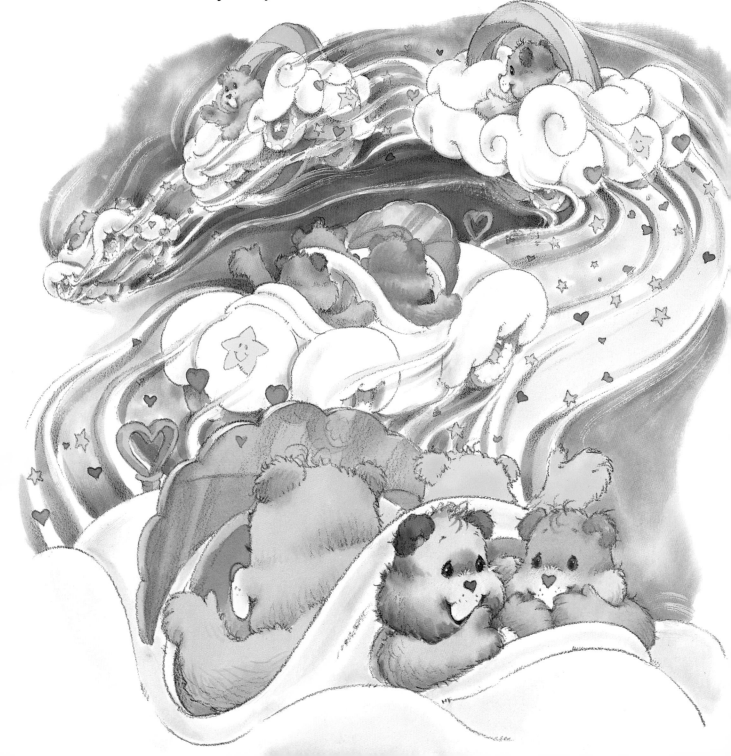

As the Care Bears sped to earth, Cold Heart sped off to his hidden mansion where he was building his "Care-less Ray Contraption."

"Frostbite!" he shouted. "Come here, now!"

Into the laboratory walked his assistant, who could not seem to stop shivering.

"Is the machine fixed?" demanded Cold Heart.

"It's all r-r-ready," answered Frostbite.

"Good," said Cold Heart. "Now we can numb the kiddies' spirits and freeze their little hearts. Start the Contraption!"

Frostbite pressed a button. There was a clanging, a banging, a pinging and a ringing.

And then a big explosion.

Cold Heart screamed, "You've ruined my Care-less Ray Contraption, you fool!" He stamped his feet and glared at Frostbite. Then suddenly he began to smile. "Wait a minute, I have a wonderful, coldhearted idea. That boy, Paul, knows a lot about machines. He could probably fix my Contraption. Find him, Frostbite, and bring him here."

Paul was still feeling bad as he walked by the playground. He hated it when the other kids called him "oddball." He wanted to have other kids like him. He swore that he'd make that Lumpy pay for what he had done.

Over his shoulder he heard a voice say, "You won't make any friends with that look on your face."

Paul looked and saw all the Care Bears.

"Who are you?" he asked.

"We're the Care Bears," Tenderheart answered. "We've come to be your friends."

Paul sighed, "I don't have any friends."

"Anyone would be your friend if you just showed that you care," said Friend Bear.

"Yes," agreed Funshine. "And you shouldn't strike out in anger, no matter what Lumpy did to you. In fact, you..."

But Frostbite interrupted this conversation by poking his head around a tree and whispering to Paul, "Never mind what they say. Just w-w-watch this."

Over in the playground, Lumpy was waiting
for a pitch. As the ball came toward him, Frostbite
whistled and the bat turned into a giant icicle.
When the ball hit it, the bat shattered.

Paul and Frostbite almost fell over laughing.

"That's n-n-nothing," said Frostbite. "Let's go and have some real f-f-fun."

As they started to leave, Tenderheart Bear called out to Paul, "What about making friends?"

"It's too late," said Paul.

"It's never too late if you care enough," shouted all the Care Bears. But Paul was already gone.

Good Luck Bear spoke up, "This is really serious. This calls for a Care Bear conference."

They climbed back into their cars, but Baby Hugs and Baby Tugs, who had gotten out to see if they could help, were too slow, and the Cloud Cars left without them. They watched helplessly as the others disappeared. "Oh Tugs, what will we do now?" asked Hugs.

Back at the conference in Care-a-Lot, the Care Bears decided that it wasn't enough to *tell* Paul that he should try to reach out and make friends.

"We have to *show* him that he can make friends for himself," said Friend Bear.

Just then Grams Bear rushed in. "Hugs and Tugs are lost," she said. "I think they may have gone off with you, but they didn't come back."

"We'd better find them right away," said Grumpy Bear as they all started to leave. "Let's go back to where we last saw Paul. Maybe they are still there."

But while the Care Bears were in Care-a-Lot,
Professor Cold Heart had spied the two deserted
Baby Bears.

"It looks like hunting season on fuzzy-wuzzies
has just begun," he cackled.

Holding on to each other, the Baby Bears tried
not to be afraid. Baby Tugs said bravely, "I'm not
scared of anything."

Professor Cold Heart jumped out of the bushes. "You're not?" he screeched. "We'll see about that, hee, hee, hee."

Before they could run, Professor Cold Heart snatched up the two Baby Bears and popped them into a sack. "Now let's see how coldhearted I can be," he muttered as he dragged the sack toward his mansion.

When Professor Cold Heart finally arrived at his destination, he found Frostbite showing Paul the Care-less Ray Contraption.

"Do you think you can fix it? It will help you get back at that big bully and all the others."

"You bet," said Paul.

Cold Heart added, "To make it work best, you have to make the Ray bounce off that bell in the tower before it hits its victims. Could you climb up and open the shutters a bit wider?"

Paul agreed to try. He soon fixed the Care-less Ray Contraption, and then he ran to the tower. He climbed higher and higher. Then, suddenly, a rung on the ladder broke! Paul lost his balance and was barely able to hold on.

The Care Bears had just traced Cold Heart's path as far as the tower when they heard somebody calling, "Help! Somebody help me. I'm up here."

"You're going to need some luck," said Good Luck Bear as he floated up toward Paul and handed him a four-leaf clover.

Paul caught the four-leaf clover, and it seemed
to pull him up the tower to safety. He reached the
shutters and flipped them open.

Wish Bear whispered, "I wish Paul hadn't
done that, and I wish he were on the ground."

There was a puff of smoke, and Paul stood before them.

"Oh, it's you," Paul sneered. "Don't try to tell me about friendship. Don't you understand that you just helped me get even with everybody?" And with that he ran back to Cold Heart.

Bursting into Professor Cold Heart's laboratory, Paul shouted, "I did it. Now tell me what you are going to do to Lumpy and..."

Paul stopped, speechless. In front of him was a huge block of ice with Baby Hugs and Baby Tugs frozen inside.

Cold Heart cracked a smile. "Now that my Contraption is working, I'm going to do something like that to every boy and girl in town."

When Paul saw what he had helped Professor Cold Heart to do, he was so ashamed that he fled down the stairs. Sobbing, he crawled into a dark corner.

The Care Bears heard Paul and tried to get to him. But Cold Heart saw them coming. He quickly set traps to confuse them.

They were tricked by mirrors.

And fake walls.

And trapdoors.

Grumpy Bear complained, "I'd sure like to find out where we are going."

But just then the sound of Paul's sobbing grew louder, and the Care Bears turned a corner and found him.

"Paul," said Tenderheart Bear, "what's wrong?"

"Cold Heart has frozen two Baby Bears," Paul explained. "And he's going to freeze all the kids in town. I didn't want that to happen. But now it's too late to stop him."

Tenderheart said gently, "It's never too late if you care enough."

Grumpy Bear frowned, "I don't think he cares enough."

"I do; I do care enough," shouted Paul. "Follow me!"

All the Care Bears and Paul raced around every trap and finally reached the laboratory.

"You're too late, fuzzy-wuzzies. Every child in town is frozen solid, just like these two," said Cold Heart, pointing to Baby Tugs and Baby Hugs. "There's nothing you can do to melt them."

The Care Bears began to whisper among themselves. Then they all lined up and Friend Bear announced, "It's time for the Care Bear stare."

"The Care Bear stare," cackled Professor Cold Heart. "Not this time. You're too late."

"You're wrong," said Paul. "It's never too late if you care enough."

The Care Bears all turned toward the Contraption. Tenderheart Bear gave the order: "Care Bears...Stare!"

All the Care Bears' love and caring fed into the Care-less Ray Contraption and turned it into a rainbow maker. Beautiful beams shot out and melted every frozen child in the town. Even the block of ice trapping Baby Hugs and Tugs melted.

Professor Cold Heart stamped his feet and shouted, "Drat! You've won again, Care Bears, but I'll get even next time."

"Trying to get even only adds to the problem," said Paul. "Take it from me."

"I can see that Paul has learned his lesson," said Cheer Bear. "It's time for us to head back to Care-a-Lot. There are others who will need our help."

As the Care Bears mounted their Cloud Cars, Paul stood and waved. Then he started to walk toward the school yard where the other kids were playing. It was time to start making some new friends.